FRENCH, Vivian
Christmas mouse

PET

The Royal Borough
Windsor &
Maidenhead
leisure, cultural
& property services

CLASS NO.

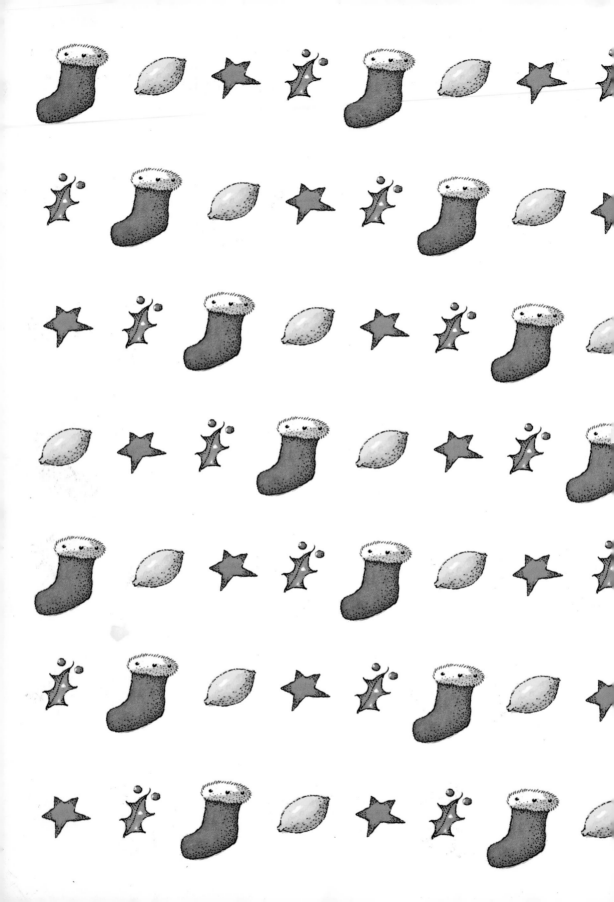

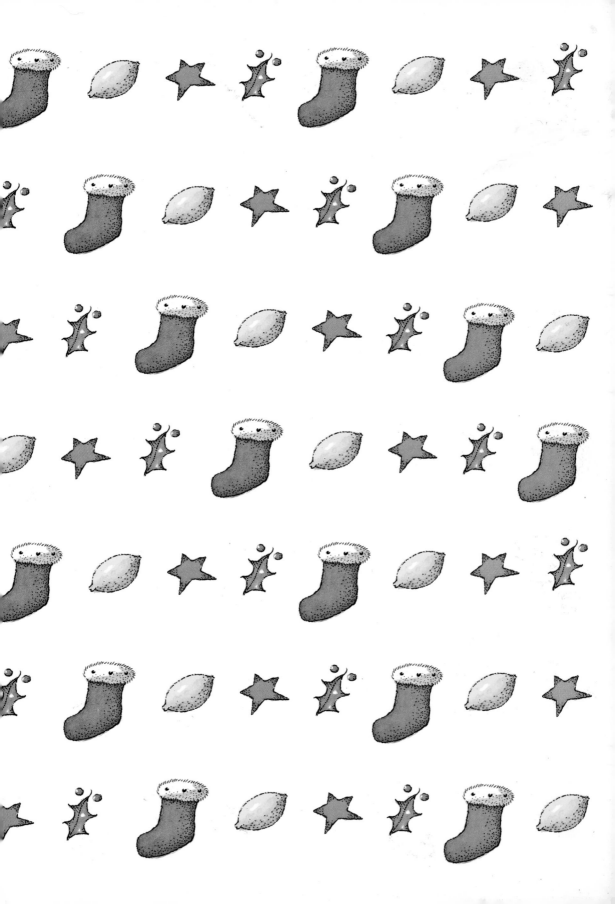

For Nancy with lots of love
V.F.
For my Mum and Dad
C.F.

First published 1992 by Walker Books Ltd
87 Vauxhall Walk, London SE11 5HJ

This edition published 2000

2 4 6 8 10 9 7 5 3 1

Text © 1992 Vivian French
Illustrations © 1992 Chris Fisher

Printed in Hong Kong

British Library Cataloguing in Publication Data
A catalogue record for this book
is available from the British Library.

ISBN 0-7445-7212-6

CHRISTMAS MOUSE

Vivian French
illustrated by Chris Fisher

WALKER BOOKS
AND SUBSIDIARIES
LONDON · BOSTON · SYDNEY

RBWM
LIBRARY SERVICES

MMAI		METO	
MWIN		METW	
MASC		MOLD	
MCOO		MSUN	
MDAT		MCON	
MDED			

It was the day before Christmas.
Mother Mouse, Dora Mouse, Middling Mouse and
the baby went to visit Grandma and Grandpa Mouse.

Grandpa had a cold, but Grandma said he was sure to be better by Christmas Day. She fetched him a hot lemon drink. Middling Mouse loved hot lemon drinks, but there weren't enough lemons for him to have one too.

Mother Mouse settled Grandpa in the comfy kitchen chair with a rug over his knees. Middling loved snuggling up under the rug, but Mother told him to play with the baby.

Dora found some paper and made Grandpa a get well card. Middling said he loved cards, but Dora said he'd have to wait until Christmas Day.

Baby Mouse climbed on to Grandpa's lap with a book.

"I'll get a book as well," said Middling.

"No room," the baby said firmly.

Middling went under the table to think.

He came out again and sneezed very loudly.

"ATCHOO! ATCHOO! ATCHOO!"

"Poor Middling," said Grandma.

"Have you got a cold too?"

Middling nodded.

"Oh dear," said Mother.

"Atchoo!" said Middling.

Mother and Dora and Middling and the baby said
goodbye to Grandpa and Grandma and hurried
through the rain back to their own house. There
was a letter on the doormat, and Mother opened it.
"How lovely!" she said. "We're invited next door for
supper tonight. Even the baby can come!"
"Hurrah!" said Dora and Middling.

"You can't come with a cold, Middling," said Mother.
"You'd better go straight to bed."
"Oh," said Middling.

Middling sat up in bed
waiting for his hot lemon
drink, but it didn't come.

He waited for someone
to come and wrap him
up in a soft woolly rug,
but they didn't.

He waited for Dora
to bring him a card,
but no card came.

And he could hear the baby laughing with Mother
in the kitchen.

Middling came back into the kitchen.
"Hello, Middling," said Mother.
"Are you feeling better?"
"Yes, and I'm hungry,"
said Middling.
"You'd better stay in just
for tonight," said
Mother. "You don't
want to be ill on
Christmas Day."
Middling opened
his mouth to say
that he was feeling
very well indeed,
but he sneezed instead.

"Oh dear," said Mother, "you
really have got a cold. You stay
here. We won't be late. Knock
on the wall if you need anything."

Mother and Dora and the baby hurried out.
Middling sat by the kitchen table and felt
sad and lonely, even though the wall was so
thin that he could hear his family arriving
next door. He ate a biscuit very slowly.

"ATCHOOOOOO!"

It was the biggest sneeze that Middling had ever heard.
And it was just outside the window… Middling didn't
know whether to hide or to go and look.

"ATCHOOOOO!" There it was again. Middling crept
to the window.

"OH!" Middling's eyes opened wide. Outside, standing
on Middling's very own garden path, was Father
Christmas – a wet, cold-looking Father Christmas.
Middling ran to the door, and flung it open.
"DO come in!" he said.

Father Christmas shivered as he came into Middling's warm cosy kitchen. "B'rrrr!" he said. "It's horrible out there! ATCHOOOOO!"
He pulled a huge white hankie out of his pocket, and blew his nose loudly. "Can't stop sneezing."

"Why don't you sit in the comfy chair?" said Middling.
"And if you don't mind pouring the hot water I'll make
  you a hot lemon drink."
"That sounds splendid," said Father Christmas.
"Exactly what I need. ATCHOOOOO!"

Middling carefully cut up
a lemon, and squeezed
it into a cup. He added
a spoonful of honey,
and then he switched
the kettle on. When it
boiled Father Christmas poured the hot water into
the cup, and sat back down in the chair with a sigh.

"Wonderful," he said. "Thank you, Alexander."
Middling looked surprised. "Nobody ever calls me that,"
he said. "They call me Middling."
"Why?" asked Father Christmas.
Middling rubbed his ear. "Well... I suppose because Dora's
bigger, and the baby's littler. I'm just a middling mouse."

"Oh," said Father Christmas. "I see. ATCHOOOOO!"

"Dear me," said Middling. "That *is* a bad cold."

He fetched a blanket from his bed, and arranged it over Father Christmas's knees. Father Christmas finished his drink, and sat back and closed his eyes. Middling found a piece of paper and a pencil and wrote out a get well card. He put it on the table and then quietly tidied away the lemon pips and skins into the rubbish bin.

Father Christmas was snoring – a gentle, comfortable snore. Middling felt tired too, and settled himself on the rug in front of the fire.

His eyes slowly closed, and he began to snore as well... a small, happy snore.

He was so fast asleep that he never heard Father Christmas stretch and shake himself awake, and he didn't stir when Father Christmas tiptoed across the room and out of the door.

Middling was woken by Mother Mouse and Dora and
the baby coming home. He stared all around the kitchen.
"Where's Father Christmas?" he asked.
"It's too early in the evening for Father Christmas.
I expect you've been dreaming," said Mother.

Middling rubbed his eyes. The card was gone from
the table... had he really been dreaming? He peeped
in the rubbish bin. The little heap of lemon skins
was still there. He smiled to himself.

"How's your cold, Middling?" Mother asked when
she kissed him good night.
"I think it's nearly gone," said Middling,
snuggling down.
"Poor Middling," said Mother. "I hope it's all gone
in the morning."

Middling woke up in the very middle of the night.
It was quite, quite dark, except for one bright star
shining in the sky outside his window.
Something – or someone – flew across the star, and
then disappeared... Middling couldn't be certain,
but he thought he heard a sneeze.

Christmas Day was bright and sunny. Middling's stocking was bulging with toys and games, and he tumbled out of bed to see what Dora and the baby had been given.

They all hurried into the kitchen to show Mother Mouse. Mother was standing at the table looking very surprised. Middling stopped and stared. The table was heaped with lemons, and on top was a parcel and a card with his name on the front. He ripped open the paper, and found the softest warmest scarf he had ever seen.

ALEXANDER

Inside the card
was a message:

With thanks to a mouse
who knows exactly how
to cure a cold. May your
whiskers always be long,
and your sneezes short.
Much love,
FATHER CHRISTMAS xx
P.S. Very Happy Christmas.

Mother Mouse looked at Middling. "Whatever were you doing last night?"

Middling sniffed at a lemon. "Only curing a cold."

Mother Mouse gave him a hug. "Well, a mouse who gets a special present from Father Christmas must be a special mouse, not just a middling mouse. I think we'd better call you Alexander from now on." And Alexander put on his scarf and began his Very Happy Christmas.

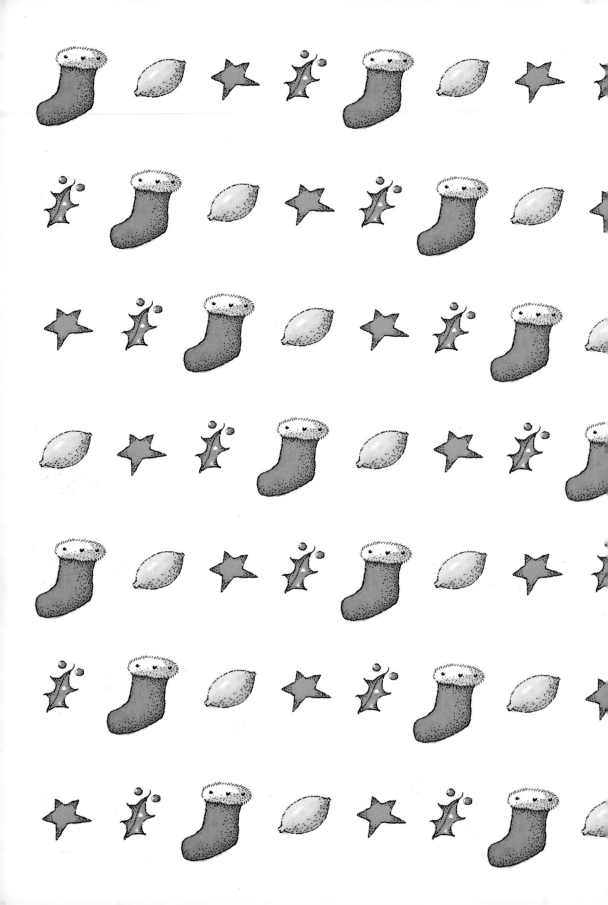

Christmas Mouse

VIVIAN FRENCH has particular empathy with the small hero of *Christmas Mouse*. She says, "I'm in the middle – I have an older brother and a younger brother – and I think being a Middling Mouse is very hard work!"

Vivian worked in children's theatre for ten years as both an actor and writer, before becoming an acclaimed children's author and storyteller. Her picture books include *Please, Princess Primrose!*, *A Song for Little Toad* (shortlisted for the 1995 Smarties Book Prize), a retelling of *A Christmas Carol* and the non-fiction titles *Caterpillar Caterpillar* (shortlisted for the Kurt Maschler Award) and *Growing Frogs*. She has also written many fiction titles for young readers. She lives in Edinburgh.

CHRIS FISHER was immediately drawn to the warmth of *Christmas Mouse*, and finds it a very comforting story. He thinks its appeal lies in the familiarity of its setting: like many Christmas stories it begins on Christmas Eve. "But the difference with this Christmas story," he says, "is that it's raining, just like the Christmases we've had for the past few years."

Chris Fisher did a BA Honours Degree in Fine Art at Newcastle Polytechnic. He then spent several years working for the Bristol Playbus Project as a community arts worker and for the social services as a careworker with mentally and physically disabled people. Among his many collaborations with Vivian French are the picture book *Please, Princess Primrose!* and the story collections *Under the Moon*, *The Boy Who Walked on Water* and *The Thistle Princess and Other Stories*. Chris lives in Bristol and enjoys music, sport and eating too much.

ISBN 0-7445-6941-9 (pb)

ISBN 0-7445-6021-7 (pb)

ISBN 0-7445-5299-0 (pb)